Overcast with Sunbreaks
Stories and Poems of Oregon

By June Reynolds
Photos by June Reynolds

Illustrated by Clyde List

Overcast with Sunbreaks: Stories and Poems of Oregon

Library of Congress Control Number: 2022902456
ISBN: 978-1-945587-75-7

1. Short story
2. Poetry
3. Essay
4. Oregon

Photos: June Reynolds
Illustrations: Clyde List
Book Design: Dancing Moon Press
Cover Design: Dancing Moon Press

Dancing Moon Press
Bend, Oregon USA
dancingmoonpress.com

Contents

Introduction: The Climate of Oregon Overcast with Sunbreaks

Two thirds of the year in Oregon, the weather is overcast. Fall and spring days usually start off dark and foggy, then by afternoon, there are "sunbreaks." For a dozen years, weather people were always saying "Tomorrow will be overcast with sunbreaks." I think they said it so much that people started complaining. However, it is very descriptive of many things in the state of Oregon. Things can be dark, cold, and dull. But with a puff of wind and a porthole of blue, the spirit can soar. This is the theme of this collection of short stories and poems.

This book started out as a collection of stories and impressions of the past and present. However, by March 2020, a world-wide pandemic came into our lives. At first, I was not going to write about the subject, but as time dragged on, I could not help it. Our microcosm of the world may have been limited, but the natural world moved on as if nothing had happened. So, this book has become two books in one: that of things pre and post covid. Most of the names in this book are made up, except for historically significant names of important people.

Winter is a very gray affair all the time, but people get so used to the gray that they ignore it. They also ignore rain as well. But when that gray material parts, there are "blue breaks" that widen into a full summer of happiness.

I am a weather watcher all the time. I love to watch the sky and all the drama of the wind and rain breaking into a symphony. This outside movement of wind and water infect the people of this state. It is our meditation waterfall. Despite the gloomy overcast weather outside, it is the glorious memories of those "sunbreaks" that shine in the mind.

Tabla Rosa

The blank page. So simple and beautiful-- before you scribble all over it.

The blank calendar. Pretty seasonal picture on top of open squares, which are all staring at me and asking for information.

Open meadow, surrounded by high forested ridges in the central coast range of Oregon. An etch-a-sketch of land erased many times by humans, grown back up with bushes and trees that grow like weeds, and renewed once again by rain in the wilderness.

This is where we start. This is where we end. All things old made new again.

Camped in the Coast Range

June 19, 2019

L.L. "Stub" Stuart; photo from Oregon State Legislature

We are camped in L.L. Stub Stewart campground on the east side of the Coast Range. This logging area is preserved for citizens to enjoy by an Oregon logging legend who was raised in logging camps, himself. His father was an old logging boss and he and his brother built and ran Bohemia Logging Co. which employed thousands of workers. "Stub" also spent 40 years advising the Oregon Parks and Recreation Department and was an Oregon State legislator from 1951 to 1955. He left this land and left us all in 2005. "Widow Maker Trail," the "Barber Chair" and "Bark Spud Trail" give us a glimpse of logger lingo.

It is an overcast morning, but pretty warm. There is no threat of rain. There is no wind. It is a mighty humid summer day. A ridge beyond us, displays additional fog, spilling over the mountains and trees. Above that, there is a second gray wall of clouds. Cloud watching is one of my favorite camping activities.

Suddenly there is a rustle in the lower treeline. We watch to see what might happen. Slowly a young doe comes tiptoeing out of the trees. She looks both ways. She makes slow movements forward. Behind her is a real loud rustling of brush.

She turns and gives a little soft bleat. *Maw*. Out pops two little speckled fawns. They start to dance in front of their mother. Someone in the upper layer of the camp slams a car door. The babies freeze and their mother's ears fold back. She will bolt at any moment, back into the tree line. Nothing happens and the deer family slowly head to the water faucet. There is a rock that is dished right there and the deer get a drink. Then they wander out of sight.

I look up at the cobalt blue wall of clouds. You can almost see a blurry rainbow. The ridge with the crawling fog from the ocean is white in contrast. Slowly the hazy rainbow in the wall becomes a rainbow ball of light. Rainbow colors are not organized by any stripes of color or curves, just random cotton candy texture. The rainbow ball begins to grow. From the east, the sun breaks over the clouds in that direction. The wall has a rainbow cast all across it. The sun is warm and the wind picks up. The light show is not distinct anymore and the glowing sun parts the gray wall to the west. The once, overcast sky opens before my eyes. The coast fog sinks away into the canyons. "The weatherman was right," states Carl. "It's going to be overcast with sunbreaks. Let's get ready to hike."

Rain Dreams

June 2018

"It's raining...raining...raining." I wake to this mournful sound. "Raining." That is not me but someone else. The room is a velvet black. The sound is coming from the ceiling. My window is open, and the wind and rain is blowing and splattering against the apartment walls. I don't get up to close the window, but I keep listening.

"Raining...raining." The ghostly voice is moaning. "Now I can't mow the lawn. Too wet. Too wet. NO, I refuse. Too wet to mow the lawn."

My mom is telling me this dramatic story. I watch her as she tells it. She is sort of in a trance, but then she opens her eyes and looks straight at me.

"Now that it is fall and it is raining almost every night, I hear this forlorn call," my mother said.

I laugh. "Oh! That is funny."

"It's not funny at 3:00 am in the morning," Mom points out. "There is a lady that lives right above my bedroom and the next-door neighbor. She carries on for a half an hour or so and I can't get back to sleep."

"This is why people believe in ghosts," I said, musing. "People say crazy things in their sleep."

Mom frowns. "I saw her, or rather heard her, the other day in the dining room. That's how I knew it was her. Her voice, that is. I think that since I have lost my sight, my hearing has gotten better. Not in volume, but in just the sound—the tone, if you know what I mean."

"Of course," I agreed. We started talking about something else.

*****

"If you do not mow the lawn today, I'm going to do it myself!" yells the lady upstairs. Well, she really told someone off, I think to myself. I look at my clock. I can barely make out 2:30 am. I hear the next-door neighbor open the door, then it quietly closes. "The grass grows when it rains...raining...raining...raining..." Now it is quiet. The neighbor comes back into his apartment, as quietly as possible. The door clicks.

It is blessedly quiet. Then suddenly: "No, No, No!" she yells again. "You will mow the grass rain or shine! I insist!"

The man next door shouts: "Shut the heck up!" He thumps the ceiling with a broom handle. There is blessed silence.

"Well, my rain complainer is at it again," my Mom says wrapping up her dramatic story.

Now things seem to be getting out of control. "I think you'd better complain to the staff here."

My Mom hedges: "Well I did talk to her twin sister."

"She has a twin sister?" I say dully. "How do you know?"

"Table-talk at dinner," Mom says. "I went over to talk to the sister and she says the lady in 215 talks in her sleep. That is why the sister moved to a different room."

*****

"I hate hate hate it here. I want to go baaaack to the farm!" It is 3:30 am. I am suddenly wide awake again. "Raining...raining...raining...Time to go back to the farm. It is flooding! Suddenly someone slams the hall door really loud. The whole building shakes. It is quiet.

"Our lady upstairs wants to go back to her farm," Mom reports. She looks tired this afternoon. I stood up. "I'm going to complain to the management." My mom shakes her head. "No one is there. They are all out this week."

"What? Who is running this place, anyway?"

My mom looks at me and says: "I think it is the cook in the kitchen."

*****

"I need NEED sun! No, I don't want to mow the lawn—You do it!" It is 2:00 am. She is at it again. "I am going away...away from

here." Now she is singing. "I am going away from here. I am going to Arizona! Arizona!!!"

My mom has two blissful months of peace.

*****

"Get out the snowplow—start up the snowmobiles," commanded a voice from upstairs. I sit up in shock! It is 3:00 am again. I had no idea she was back. Our 'night yeller' as the neighbors so laughingly called her has dreamed of a new chapter in her life. She was at it again. According to her sister, it was when she lived up in Maine on the East coast. Every night they were mobilizing for snow. "It's drifting, drifting, drifting along..." she sang.

Mom wasted no time continuing the story. "By now, the man next door had an agreement with the staff that he would pull the emergency buzzer three times to alert the staff. This has been going on for four nights now."

*****

I walked by the office and saw that one of the administrators was there. I walked in. "Uh, hi. I was wondering what you folks are going to do with the lady in 215 who yells in the middle of the night. My mom needs her sleep."

She smiled a winning grin. "We are aware of the situation and we are going to solve the problem. At the same time, we are having another reduction in staff. We will no longer have a person on night duty."

"So how is that going to solve your problem?" I demanded.

She fake-smiled again. "We are going to negotiate with the family to move this lady to the bottom floor in the east wing where we have no other residents on either side and the beauty shop on the second floor.

The next time I came to visit mom, she had good news: "Our sleep talker has finally moved to the east wing!"

"Wow that is really great, mom."

Mom did not smile. "We also lost our person on night staff. Quite frankly, I think he got fed up and quit."

[Photo by Dave Gilmore]

Moon's Night Out

The Moon hops up the mountain top
To see what he can see.
It's Friday night he is a sight,
He's on a playing spree.
He swings through clouds and shining stars
On his night trapeze.
He's very round and very full,
And slightly hard to please.

He wines and pines, 'cause there's no signs
of anything to do.
Then he rolls to bowl the kingpin nines.
And glows some light to pool.

He settles down to a video game, but soon he has to frown.
TIME IS UP! The rooster crows.
The Moon must climb back down.
He waves and winks, as he thinks I'll see you all around.

Cold Fish

(This is a futuristic, cautionary tale of animals gone awry. Oh, woe the new-found animal. We should have been more careful with our environment...)

I found myself at the Oregon Coast on the beach of my childhood, possibly near Rockaway Beach. In those days, the beach houses looked more like whitewashed shacks, all tilted at angles in the drifted sand. The sky was a very blue backdrop to the creamy white hillocks and the peeling white buildings. The windows were curtained by faded multi-colored beach towels. Everything looked old and worn.

Suddenly I heard a squeaking of moving metal and

a screech of metal on metal in measured rhythms. It was sounding from the side of the tilted shack. I looked around to the building to see some ungodly thing moving up and down, up and down, up and down bearing towards me.

"What the heck is that?" I exclaimed.

"A cold fish," said a deadpan reply. I jumped. My son was beside me. I did not realize anyone was near me.

The old thing gleamed in the sun. It was an old walker, long ago abandoned by an immobile elder, which was now humping its way up a sandy ridge. When it got to the top of the ridge, it looked to one side in profile and I realized the unreal creature had a yellow plastic bowl attached on a stick for a "head" and a pair of barbeque tongs for a "beak." They would snap from time to time. "Who made that? How does that work? "I asked.

My son, who is an addict for science and nature programs on TV, continued his commentary. "This is called a cold fish. He's like a hermit crab who gets in a shell or whatever in which to live." It is a protoplasm within a hardened shell.

"The dead fish gets into the walker?" I asked.

My son laughed. "Yep. But the fish is not dead. He is alive. He fills all voids in the seat and the tubing. He is a viable new life form. He is a modern adaptation of nature. They are called cold fish."

My mouth flew open as I gasped. "That is just too creepy."

He sighed. "It's the way of our world now; it's not too bad yet. But when these garbage islands move in off the ocean and onto our beaches, we may be in for a big surprise. Our President does not believe it is happening."

Suddenly something came crashing over a dune on the other side of the shack. It looked like this thing was following the first cold fish who just kept on moving out to the ocean. This new, crashing cold fish looked more like a rust bucket, revolving on three legs, flapping a grill off the side. It was faded red and I realized it was an entire barbeque. The lid was ajar, and several skewers were sticking out of what could be imagined as a mouth.

This piece of junk somehow knew we were there because he revolved very close to us, scraped up a spatula of sand, and reached out to offer it to us.

My son pushed the spatula away and said, "No thank you." The rust bucket turned to me and offered me the spatula of sand. My son stifled a laugh as I nodded and said, "Thank you, sir." The cold fish dumped the sand back on the beach and continued its revolving down to the beach. Both cold fish then continued into the surf until it washed over them, and they floated away.

Evolution at the Bay

But the story did not stop, for the next day, I was down at the Alsea Bay. It is a small bay which snakes around and has a strong bar as the river water pushes out into the ocean. There are plenty of deep pools and sandy bar for the seals at low tide.

I went up to the docks, not far upriver from the bay. At the end of the street there you could park and rent some crab pots and get crabs right off the dock during the right season. I rented a couple of crab pots and some bait and the guy at the dock sort of looked at me funny. He shook his head and took my money.

I was pretty excited as I flung my first crab pot into the bay. It plunged right down then drifted a bit under the dock. I managed to get the second crab trap farther out and it swung out towards the ocean. Off in the distance, I could see a white object. It started sailing right at me from the center of the current. That seemed a little strange. In no time at all, the white thing was bobbing right in front of me. It zipped right up to the dock and submerged.

The day was three shades of blue and was dazzled by twinkling water sparkles. A faint breeze made the water choppy and the American flag waved a limp flap.

Kersploosh! A slap of water washed onto the dock and the white lumpy thing exploded up out of the water with my crab pot! The crab pot was empty.

Now I could see this white lumpy thing clearly. It was a mass of gallon milk jugs somehow lashed together with wire, rubber bands string, barbed wire, long grass and yarn. There were masses of pink guts in those jugs. It was a colony of cold fish. I cringed at the sight of the pink squirming guts and realized that this mass of protoplasm with a mild jug shell had just sucked the bait out of my crab pot. No wonder the dock guy looked at me funny when I said I was going to get crabs for dinner!

"Pretty pathetic crabbing, right?" said someone behind me. I jumped, but it was only my son, the nature lover, again. He was drinking from a glass soda bottle. I looked at the milk jug mass bobbing right off the dock.

My stomach turned as I took a stick and pushed it back away from the dock.

"The ocean is so full of garbage that it is choking the natural flow of life. Now life is in garbage and soon it will overtake humans." He said grimly. "There will be no life on the water, except for cold fish and, as you have seen on the beach, the cold fish are evolving onto land like the first animals long ago."

"People do not believe that there is climate change or that the oceans are engulfed with garbage," I said

My son coughed. Little pink protoplasm balls fell out of his mouth. He said: "We have missed the boat…missed the boat... missed the boat."

"Wake up Grandma! We are going to miss the boat!" The voice was my grandson, by the bedside. We were going out on a fishing boat. The whole sickening story was really a dream, but could it really happen? It already is...

Bees on a Plum Tree

March 27, 2021

Honeybees with their saddle pouches,
On legs budging, they are no slouches.
Sweet smell calls them, it is delicious.
Wafting in heat, the sun so auspicious.
Bees bend in their work, a-flower,
On this fleeting Bluebird Day.
We cast our eyes into the skies a memory to replay.

A Universe of Possibilities

We enter the library for the first time this summer. It has sort of been a gray day, so I am glad there is a place for us to go. By the time we get to the children's area, the sun comes out and shines through the beautiful window of the children's section. It is not the first time we have enjoyed the view. We saw a double rainbow from one end to the other out that window. "Dat was the best Elbow we ever saw, huh, Grandma?" remembers Ahny.

It is getting to be afternoon so the sun beams in at a slant over at the tall bookcase and Bobby goes running to the display. "Tars Tars," says Bobby in his best library tone. Sure enough, there is a silhouette of a boy on a cardboard stand-up with a telescope looking at the stars. Bobby wants to go to space. Bobby is four going on two, but he knows a thing or three. "Tars" he says. He is saying this to me and as he turns to look around, he sees something else! His eyes widen and he grins.

A small sliver of light is cast across the room to a bookcase with a silhouette figure of a girl, pointing to space. He runs to her. In one fell swoop, he gets on tiptoe and grabs her from the shelf. He is barely tall enough to do this, but he does it quite successfully. The cardboard is as big as his whole body. I watch him carefully, so that he doesn't wreck anything. No one else notices and I want to see what he is going to do. This is a kid who has not had much freedom in his life, so I give him some slack. He waddles the cardboard figure over to the figure of the boy, being very careful. He puts her carefully, on the floor. He looks at the boy. Ahny, Bobby's brother asks me a question and I turn to answer him. In a flash, there is Bobby, scaling the bookshelf! I leap into action and bring him down. "No, Bobby you are not to climb the bookshelf."

He looks at me. He looks at the cardboard on the floor. He points at it, then he points to the boy, above. "Tars." He says sadly. The two figures belong together but were placed on either side of the room. Bobby wants to put them together. I carefully put the girl up on the shelf with the boy. Bobby looks pleased. "They have to stay there, Bobby. Stay together." I put his hands together. Bobby thinks about it and decides I am right. He goes to a new activity with the Itsy-Bitsy Spider. The next week, the boy and girl are still on the bookcase together.

Overcast Day

The arc of time is slowed to a pause
As the clouds grow knuckled, flexing their paws.
To some, a sign of sad, old grief.
To others, drops of pure relief.
Then, port holes of blue—such winks from above.
Which give hope for growth or even some love.

Fair Play

By Lyle Kent

It all happened in a flash of time. I was sitting there at the ballpark at Hopkins School. It was one of those strangely warm emerald June days, watching Teddy play T-Ball. Teddy was in the 5-year-old group, even though he just turned 6 so he was the brute of the team. The boys were all bumbling around on the field, barely able to keep their positions. There were several big softballs being flung in the air and bouncing on kid's heads.

Two adult men were in charge, I guess, so they were running around showing each boy what to do. Sort of re-enacting the game. As the ball would trickle off the T by some power- house of a 5-year-old batter, one adult would rush the boy to the base while the other adult grabbed a first baseman or shortstop and hustle them over to the ball and then try to throw it. Some balls had to be thrown three times before maybe the batter was safe. One boy resisted the coach and yelled out: "Don't touch me!"

At the same time the two adult coaches were verbally battling with each other. (Talk about multi-tasking!!)

"You are such a loser!" said number one. "Wilsonville never won state the whole time you went there! It's a hit! Try pitching lower, Billy."

Number two dumped his batter down on the base. "Oh yeah? Well, at least Wilsonville came into the playoffs and only lost to Sherwood by one run!"

The man put his hands on his hips, releasing his boy, "Run Aaron! To second base. NO! That is first base! The other base!" The boy stood there befuddled. "So you got second at State, Mr. Wilsonville, second is for looooosers!"

"Wilsonville is way better at all sports than Tigard, that's for sure!" shouted the second one.

"Does that include the girls' sports?" asked the Tigard High guy.

"Speaking of girls sports," said Wilsonville High, "Why do you drive an old beat-up 1983 Chrysler?"

"That's a vintage collectors-item!" hollered Tigard High. "Why don't you get a bigger vehicle to haul the kids in? Or are you too stuck up with your Mini-Cooper?"

"I...bleep'en...QUIT!" screamed the Wilsonville High guy. He stomped away from the diamond.

"Well, I quit too!" said Tigard High guy, who stomped off, leaving his kid in the outfield.

"Dad, Dad, wait for me," said the pathetic little boy in center field. He had a long way to run.

The father kept on walking, then in a blind rage, he pushed a random kid dancing on the edge third base.

"Dad!" screamed the little outfielder. "You forgot me!"

I jumped up and went out to second base and told the little boy to follow his dad to the car. He did this, and as I walked back, I stood surrounded by ten little boys, including Teddy, who all needed some love. Two moms hung back, very involved with their new I-Phones, but most of the parents were not there and were gone with hopeful wishes that someone was watching their kids in a responsible manner.

"Let's sit down in a circle," I told the boys with questioning eyes. I did not know what to tell them.

After a moment, Teddy piped up: "Let's play Duck, Duck, Goose!"

"Yay," cheered all the boys. They all knew how to play and we all had a good time for a blissful forty-five minutes. Then all the parents came and claimed their kids.

As Teddy and I were gathering up the balls and bats, a barrel-chested man ambled over from another diamond, chuckling: "Hey, kid, ha ha, hey, you kid...looks like you are the new T-ball coach for the 'Kittens.' I've been watching this team for a few weeks, waiting for something to happen. What's your name, son?"

"My name is Lyle Kent." I looked at him, then looked down at the ground, mumbling: "Uh, well at least I got to be coach for today. I am only a kid."

"Ah, no matter, high school age is okay. All you have to do is show up at the times and dates on the schedule. Looks like you already have a little man." He wrote some stuff on his clipboard and winked at me.

"He's my brother."

The man's two-barrel chested kids came trotting from the other diamond to join the conversation.

"Everything's packed, Dad," said the big one who was almost as tall as me.

"Thanks, son," winked the guy as he tousled the little one's cornstalk of hair. Then he was right back to the main conversation.

"Those two guys are worthless as coaches. They care more about their cars and their great high school careers than they do about their kids. I know because I went to school with them and played on the Sherwood football team. The kids are better off without them."

I looked up at the guy. "Uh yeah, but I don't know how..."

"Just play games with the kids, like you did today. Have them play catch at two feet away, and as they get better, make them take a step back. Line 'em all up and have them hit the ball off the T. When they get good, if they hit the ball, make them run to first. Later on, to second and third and home. Make everything a game and their skills will get better. You probably won't even have to play a real game all season." He winked at me again. "Come on, give it a try. I'm on the board and need some help...please." He looked right in my eyes and was pretty convincing.

He handed me some papers to fill out from his clipboard and that is how I became a T-ball coach.

We drove back home, and Teddy shot into the house ahead of me. When I came in, Teddy announced: "...And I hit a home run!" I shook my head "no" at Mom, who was trying not to laugh.

Grandpa, with his supersonic radar ears heard the remark from the front room with the TV blaring and said: "What? My Teddy? Hit a home run? Come to Grandpa and I'll give you a candy. A homer deserves a Candy!"

Teddy danced triumphantly into the living room and was the sports hero all night.

The Next Week

The next Saturday, I was all fired up about playing baseball games. But before we could even get started, one little boy was crying pathetically. "What is wrong, Sean?" I said as carefully as possible, away from the rest of the boys. I knew how crying could be contagious with the other kids.

He sniffled and said: "My dog, Ammo, died. He had a backstroke."

I wrapped my mind around that for a second, then realized he meant a heart attack. Quietly I said: "Listen, Sean your dog has died and has gone to a better place."

"Where is that?" asked Sean.

"All dogs go to Disneyland," I said. "People go to Heaven which is a people's Disneyland. My dad died and I like to think that he is watching me from heaven. I bet your dog could be watching you too."

That brightened him up. He wiped his face on his sleeves. "Well then, I need to show him that I can play baseball."

With that, we paired up to play catch.

The Final T-Ball Game

After a few weeks, "The Kittens T-Ball Team" was getting pretty good, even though I say so myself. All the boys could hit the ball off the T and they were able to run all three bases. The kids were getting so good that I could tell they were getting bored. I saw that the other coaches would get out and field the ball, so I started doing that too. I would try to get them "out" but many times the little boys would start to cry.

I called the boys in for a talk. "This is the next step for you guys to go on to play real baseball," I explained. "If you don't get to the base and step on it, you are out. In real baseball, you have to make it to all three bags of the diamond."

Teddy waved his hand in the air. "What about homeruns?" He was always concerned about the homerun.

"Okay." I stood up. "Home run is when you hit the ball off the T, HARD, and I cannot get you out on first base and you run all the way around to where you hit it off the T. You all can try to hit homeruns. That means you have to hit the ball hard, way out there to the grass."

They all agreed that they could do that.

So we lined up again to the T and I got in the infield. Every single kid powered that ball way out to the grass. Every single one. Their performance before that was just pitiful.

As we were getting ready to go, one of the coaches came over. "Wow!" he exclaimed. "I can't believe what I just saw! Your kids are champs! How about a friendly game next week?"

"Uh, well, sure. One line up against another line up. Points for coming home and if there is a tie, we do it again." We shook on it.

Needless to say, we had a great time, and we did tie, but the final, final score was Kittens-22/Bulldogs-19. My coaching career was over.

Speak Kindly

Speak kindly with not a piece of you in there.
Offer wisely with real help, not hollow hope.
Play willingly, long and hard with Joy.
Love longingly, both constant and with care.
Lead firmly, but with softness in your heart for those you are leading.
Act equally in every way for man, woman, and beast.
Speak kindly like a poem from your heart.

Time Capsule: The American "Self-Made" Man/Woman

I was sitting at my desk with a tattered, crumbling piece of newspaper in my hands. There was no date, but my guess is that it was from the late 1920s or 1930s. It was not a local Tualatin Valley newspaper, but possibly a state-wide paper like *The Oregonian* or *Oregon Journal*. The torn-out article was a brief interview about Gustave Hanke, Sherwood, Oregon's shoemaker. Suddenly the phone rings and I startle at the sound. I did not even say "hello."

The phone caller started right in: "Hello? Hello? June, I'm not disturbing you, am I?" asked the breathless voice of Margaret Umland. She was always busy on the farm, so I knew she just came in from the barn.

"Oh, no. I'm just looking at an old newspaper about Gustave Hanke," I said.

Margaret let out a gust of pure glee. "Oh, I just loved old 'Pops Hanke' he would be in his shop sitting on his stool in his shiny leather apron, and you would open the door and the little bell would jingle as you shut the door and Pops would look up over his glasses, and look at you, with nails in his mouth, and say 'Helwlo wee one. Wath can I do for you?' With nails in his mouth, can you believe it! It was a wonder he didn't swallow them!

An image floated before my eyes. "I remember my Grandma Wells doing the same thing with straight pins when she was sewing. So, Margaret, what can I do for you?" I asked.

"I remember that Pops made medicine out of things he picked in the woods and gave the medicine to the children for coughs. Can you just see someone doing that today?"

"No. Everyone would be suing him for that!" I laughed. I looked back down at the yellowed paper. "I only have this scrap of newspaper. I can't make this out here…something about Mr. Hanke being in charge of entertainment."

"Oh yes he was the superintendent of entertainment for the 4th of July Festival, except in 1913, when it was canceled because of a brawl. That was the talk of the town for many years. He was in charge of the Vaudeville Show and dressed up his own kids for the pageant. The movie, *Robin Hood* was all the rage and the song "Oh Promise Me" always had to be in the show. He's buried near Bluetown, you know, that's over at Maple Lane Cemetery. He was on the board of trustees for the place because he was a member of the East Bluetown Lutheran Church on the hill near Four-corners. You know where that's at don't you?"

"The Church was where the Sherwood School District office is today, right?"

She was delighted. "Yes! That's right."

"Well, Ms. Umland, did you have a question or something?" I asked again.

"Oh dang! I forgot! Well, when I think of it again, I'll call you back up, Okay?" she asked.

"Of course, Margaret, call me any time. I love talking to you. You are a wealth of information." And with that the phone clicked off.

I turned to my newspaper. There was someone interviewing him later in the column.

"How did you become a cobbler, Mr. Hanke?"

"As a small child, my family gave me over to be an indentured

servant. I believe they were paid money for this. I did not live with my family, but in the shoe shop. I learned the skills to make shoes. I had to make a certain number of shoes or I would get no supper."

"What was the supper like?"

"It was cabbage soup or navy beans and the like. Sometimes bread or potatoes. It was always served at midnight."

"Why did you leave Germany?

"Because I was 21 and free to be my own cobbler, but I was going to be pressed to join the compulsory army, so I made a move to leave."

"When did you come to Oregon?"

"July 5th 1891. I remember because it was the day after the 4th of July and people were still celebrating in the saloons. I walked down the sidewalk and one of the men was thrown out the door. I helped him get up and took him home. He got me a job the next day at the livery stable."

"What would be your words of wisdom for living in Sherwood?"

"Don't leave your groceries on the porch or the pigs will get them."

This got me thinking. What could be more American than the self-made man or woman? Thousands of people in Europe were like Mr. Hanke. Given over for a price by their own parents with the hope that their children would learn trades to give them a better life. In all the material that we have on Gustave Hanke, there is never any further information about his parents or his family. He made a decision to leave for America when he had a chance to break from one form of slavery to hopefully not another. After casting around, he found a wife, had a child, and was able to come to Oregon. He plied his trade and worked as a farm laborer when he needed more money. This story could be told about every other person who came to Oregon from 1859 to 1900, and even today.The pioneers and settlers not only came from an old country, but also extended themselves into the unknown land of the West. What faith these people had to keep going for months on end with no promise that this would be the last mountain they had to climb or that desert would be the last they would pass through.

This is part of the American narrative: People finding themselves on their own, coming to America for a better life, building their own homes, having their own families, and working their own jobs. These are self-made individuals with their own life story. They all had to reinvent their life to become American. The land of the free and the home of the brave.

Our Schoolmarm

Miz Ida was our schoolmarm we honor her with this plaque....

We'd never sass this lady or sit her on a tack.

She was so kind and friendly and always had our back.

"Cause Miss Ida Wilks was our schoolmarm and them's just all the facxs...

Girl Gangs

October 4, 2020

They were at it again. The fifth-grade girl gangs were swarming the playground…agitating other girls while they played foursquare. These sinister sisters were not fighting each other but plotting and scheming together against someone else—him. The teacher, Mr. Carr.

Yes. He already knew it…by their sidelong looks at him and their quick looks away. Yesterday, he shooed one group of them away from the side of the school building where the incinerator was. He overheard their meeting:

Jessie declared: "We must stick together and be a group, like the other girls are. We are the farm girls they are the town girls. We are the 'Crumbs'." Their backs were toward him as he approached so he could hear what they were saying.

Tommie piped up: "Karen wants to join us."

"Karen? Really? Why?" asked the girls all at once. Karen was from town, but her dad was a teacher and a coach.

"She does not like what they say about us," said Billie, looking down to the ground and drawing something with her foot in the gravel.

Jesse, the ringleader said after some thought: "Well, I say she can join us, if she wants. Does anyone say no?"

They all said yes.

I approached the clutch of fifth graders. "You girls are not supposed to be over here at the incinerator," I said with authority.

"Well, then the meeting of the 'Crumbs' is officially over!" said Jesse. I took a few steps and the girls scattered to the four-corners of the playground.

I had to smile. Why would any parent in their right

mind name their girls Jesse, Jerri, Billie, and Tommi? Wishful thinking, I suppose, hoping that they would turn out to be good farmhands anyway.

The new gang, "The Crumbs," started before the Columbus Day Storm of 1962. The storm halted their activities for five weeks because so many trees were down on the canyon roads. The farms did not have any electricity to pump water from the wells, so the farm people had to draw it from the old wells, creeks, and springs. None of the girls handed in their US History paper, except Jesse who poetically likened her adventure with the storm, to that of Abraham Lincoln, writing each night from a dripping candle, which was all over her paper.

Farm kids were a handful to teach, that was for sure. They were very independent and many of them knew things that were way over their heads. The town kids were more docile and innocent. The farm kids helped run the farm and were on an equal basis with their parents. They made more independent decisions on their own. Of course, the boys were favored. The boys would try to be friendly with the girls and were rebuffed for their loving boyish passion. Farm girls could not be bothered as a delicate love of a fading flower.

"The Crumbs" wore hand me down clothes. Too big shoes, too small dresses, large coats and scarves blowing in the wind. Our school did not allow girls to wear pants, even though they wore them at home or in the barnyard. A concession was made one time for the girls when the Eastern Oregon wind brought in a snowstorm and ice. The girls were allowed to wear their pants and then change into their skirts and dresses in the restroom. Jesse wore her bootleg jeans into the classroom with her ever-present but new English Brogue stompers and got an eyeful from the rest of the class. I opened my mouth to speak but decided this was not worth the battle.

Finally, the school year was turning toward spring. The daytime dome of gray was breaking up to reveal blue sky again. On the playground, Jesse made it to server in four-square. Before serving, she looked at all the kids in the squares and all the kids lined up waiting to get into the game. "I think Mr. Carr is too mean." She proclaimed. The rest of the kids stopped talking and sucked in their air. A bird flew over the game. Suddenly, everyone started talking at once: "Shhhh! He's right over there!" "He can hear you!" He has supersonic ears!" "Do you want to stay in from recess?"

"I don't care," she said, as Mr. Carr walked away from the foursquare site to check in on the swings. "He makes us do those multiplication records and they play too fast. I don't have time to think."

Many kids agreed with that point. "I think something is going to happen on April Fool's," she warned.

The next day, Mr. Carr was reading about Robin Hood since Sherwood had a Robin Hood Festival. He began: *"The story of Robin Hood and his Merry Men is a legend; half history and half wild speculation. These tales were told 'word of mouth' and sang in the form of ballads. The first recorded mention of Robin Hood was in 1370. He lived in the northern part of England in what was a wilderness known as Sherwood Forest. Robin Hood was a heroic outlaw. He fought in the Crusades and gained skill as an archer and swordsman. While he was in the war, he may have lost his ancestral farmland and became a member of the yeoman class. He wore all green clothing to camouflage himself in the forest and farm. His mission was to rob from the rich and give to the poor.*

Mr. Carr, who had been slouching over a desk to read, went back to his lectern. "Now I want you to get out pen and paper and write a dialog between Robin Hood and someone else. Remember to use all the proper punctuation: quotes, commas, and periods. There was a couple of moans and soon everyone was scratching something out. After twenty minutes, Mr. Carr commanded: "Pens down. Line leaders collect the papers."

Jesse's hands were waving wildly at the back of the class. Mr. Carr hesitated to recognize her, but decided they had some time to kill before lunch. "Yes, Jesse."

"Why does Sherwood celebrate a bad guy who robs people?"

"Well, Jesse, it is a story about the downtrodden who need help. Robin Hood is just a story, and in those days, tricking people to get something was not that bad. They thought it was being clever. The poor people, or lower class, played around and called the behavior during that time "The Age of Misrule." The lunch bell rang.

Jesse smiled. "Thank you, Mr. Carr."

Finally, it was April 1st. Most of Mr. Carr's class were at the far foursquare court. By now, "The Crumbs" was a gang of fifteen kids, both boys and girls. Most of them had defected from the town gang. It had been a good day so far, for an April Fool's Day. Everyone was behaving.

Jesse was serving the ball. She whispered, "Okay. Right when we go in from lunch recess, I want you to stall. Lose the balls way out on the field and go after them." She served the ball and got out. The bell rang and there was lots of chaos. Jesse went into the hallway and on into the room with a tack to set on Mr. Carr's desk chair. But to her horror, someone had already put a tack on the chair! In confusion, she ran out of the classroom without anyone seeing her and went to the girl's bathroom. She was shaking in the stall, but finally got the courage to put the tack in her pocket and go back to the room. Students were milling around and Mr. Carr was getting out the multiplication records. Her heart sank. Everyone got their pencils and paper out and numbered their sheet. Jesse busied herself and watched Mr. Carr. The record started: One times one…3 times 4…7 times 9…8 times 9…5 times 5. Jesse wrote 25 and looked up. Mr. Carr was sitting down at his desk. He sat straight up, then turned deep red, then turned purple. "Who did this?" He bellowed as he stood up. "6 times 9...4 times 5 6 times 6... Everyone looked at Jesse. "Young woman," shouted Mr. Carr. "Out in the hall." Jesse could hear the record as she left the room. "7 times 4…3 times 5...

"What do you have to say for yourself?" growled Mr. Carr

"I was acting under the Age of Misrule, Mr. Carr. It is April Fool's Day, but look, I didn't do it. Someone else beat me to it. See here is the tack in my pocket."

Mr. Carr was amazed. "You expect me to believe that?"

"Yes, Mr. Carr, you should believe that." It was Waldo Ames. "I cannot stand those timed records anymore, Mr. Carr. They make me nervous and give me nightmares. Jesse talked it up, but I beat her to it."

Mr. Carr marched us down the hall saying, "Look, you are both going to the office to talk to Mr. Hopkins, and you will both be doing multiplication worksheets during recess for a week. No more misrule for you two and let's try to be a gang of one, okay?"

Do you know how old I am, Mr. Carr?
Of course, you do.
If I had not been your student.
In Fifth Grade,
How would I have ever learned how to control my ambitious creativity—
To use words that I don't even know,
Let alone how to write lovely cursive or curse the multiplication tables…
A man on an even-keel; keeping the good ship afloat.
I salute you.

Knife in the Butter

I was delivering six bags of fresh picked, crunchy arugula to the fancy Bistro in Dundee. Carl and I planted it special for this very time of year. It was salmon season and so my arugula was paired with salmon filets: an Oregon-grown delicacy, in fact in some cultures a sacred food. I loved going to the back door of the Bistro and walking into the bustling kitchen. I loved going into the walk-in cooler on an early Saturday morning. There would be bowling balls of cabbage, large, whole salmon, about ready to give you a kiss with their lips, and bundles of carrots, still with tops, flopped on the shelves.

The kitchen crew were milling around strapping on their smart black aprons and matching hats. The back kitchen had a galley lined with stainless steel that glistened in the light. Everyone was gathered around a ten-pound brick of butter. In the brick near the top end was a big chef's knife. The head chef, Martine had his hands on his hips gazing at the butter. He winked at me and gave me the go ahead to put the arugula in the cooler. But I was captivated by his stance there, looking at the brick of butter. He looked like a bowling pin about ready to tip over.

He eyed the brick in front of him again. "I have had this butter laid out for over twenty-four hours and well, now my knife is stuck!"

"Like the sword in the stone!" giggled the sous-chef. Some people laughed along until Martine glared at them. A few people tried their hand at pulling out the knife, but they were not successful. It was royally stuck.

"In-coming!!!" yelled a waitress from the front of the kitchen. From out the big picture window, you could see a big tour bus pulling up and soon a line of people was entering the Bistro. The staff scattered. Martine grabbed two of my arugula bags and ordered the dishwasher to lightly spray the greens.

He turned to me and another worker: "You two! Go get the rest of the arugula in the cooler and bring me back two of those fish." He ran to get another knife and some trays.

When we came back out, Martine realized that I was not on the staff, and he apologized. "You will get a generous tip, hang in here for a while." Then he held up his knife. "I will use Suzy, my second favorite knife, since the other one is stuck in the butter. Bill, scrounge up more butter! We must have butter!" Martine slapped the two fish on the table, belly towards him and started cutting. He had two trays of rectangle fish pieces in short order. I could see that the tour bus people were still sipping their first round of wine. Bill had what butter he could find and he and Martine moved to the stove to grill their fish. Bill was working quickly with a shaved filbert sauce.

I knew Martine was not going to pay me until he got done with this rush and so I started to contemplate the knife in the butter. There it was: a giant butter pat with a large kitchen knife stuck in it all the way to the hilt. I grabbed the handle and tried to move it down, then up. It would not budge. I gave up and looked at it some more.

Then I heard a sultry voice: "What are you looking at sweetheart? Get me out of this blubber!" I thought someone was playing a prank, but everyone was hustling their butt all over the place, while Martine was shouting orders.

"What?" I asked.

The sultry voice purred menacingly. "You heard me! Get me outta here! Lift me up, then down about twenty times then pull."

I did just what she said. I even counted twenty times before I pulled. Nothing. So I pushed down one more time, pulled up and…Voila! The knife came out of the butter!

Fifteen minutes later, Martine came to the back of the kitchen. "Bravo!!!" he shouted, "You have done the impossible! How did you do it?"

I hesitated, "Well I had some help, and I followed the directions and finally the knife came out!"

Martine laughed. "You are an Amazon, lady! I'll write you a check this time for the arugula, ten dollars tip for helping, and you can have this knife!" said Martine. "I suggest you get it sharpened at the Farmer's Market. Bring me six more bags of arugula next Thursday, we are having more tour busses early next week."

I wrapped the knife in some newspaper and took it home. I felt a compelling urge to cook from then on. I sliced cabbage into coleslaw, I sliced and diced cucumbers for relish. I sliced onions paper-thin. I carved three Halloween pumpkins, and even carved a turkey at Thanksgiving. My knife never talked to me again, but I sure did a lot of cooking!

[Photo enhanced by Barbra Butchas Bergman]

Steam Queen

In early morning peachy glow
Before the market in town
I blanched a pick of broccoli
And there before me on the mound
Of toppled trees of vegetables, lo there in vapor found
A dancing girl oh so refined in a swirling glowing gown.
She winked at me and curled her arms and then she turned around.

I picked out more toppled trees of greens, some were chartreuse.
She tap danced high her hair a-fly, then wildly cut loose.
The sun beamed in to lend more light, fiddlers lightly play,
She laughed upon her mountain top a good part of the day.

But soon the music stopped the beat.
Our Steam Queen then felt caught.
Her legs reached out in great jette into the boiling pot.
She said, "Farewell"
I said "Goodbye"
I heard a bubble pop.
We'll meet again on another day that's sunny and so hot.

Coyote Highways

We always think of the Coyote being the foil of the Roadrunner but get that out of your mind when you read this story. It is about real coyotes in the real forests of Oregon. Yes, that is right! Coyotes live in most parts of North America. They may vary in appearance in different environments, but in many ways, they remain the same. They are the wild branch of the canine family. They are revered in folklore as "the trickster."

Toppling over each other in the warm, dry, rock recess, the four little pups greet their mother. They nestle down to have their milk and they quiet their winning. The mother had parted the brush at the opening and now there was a little light at the opening. The day was getting warm. It was the first day of June. The four furry little butterballs woke up from their nursing nap and wondered what that light was. They waddled over to the opening and sniffed the air. They yipped at a cold puff of wind and rolled back to their mother.

The light left but came back for another day. Two young humans and two older ones, all on two feet hiked up to the rock butte and made a lot of noise. Momma moved to the opening to protect the pups. She sat trembling as the humans climbed the rock and rolled little rocks and dust into the den. Clearly, it was time for the pups to move out.

The next day, Mother crawled out early in the morning. The sky was clear as the sun worked its way over the hills and mountains. A patch of sunlight beamed down on the den landing and Mother stretched her body and made a coyote call. The she went back in to attend the pups.

Soon, there was a shadow dimming the sun outside and a big, moist nose poked through the opening. The pups were full of milk and asleep. They did not see this terrifying sight. But the next day, as the sun rose over the hill, they did see the nose and eyes of their father looking in. They gave a few warning yips then cringed with fear. The mother moved to the opening and emerged into the sun. Mother and Father gave their greetings.

Rugged and beautiful, the rock outcropping was a one-of a kind feature in this country. It was an extrusion of basalt that cooled very quickly about twenty thousand years ago. It was one of the newest features of Parrett Mountain.

The little ones were all in a jumble inside. One of the bold pups crawled to the opening and looked out. Father gave him a lick and backed away. It was time for the pups to come out and learn about the world.

One of the little coyotes was at the opening and tumbled out. Momma nosed him and he squinted his little eyes in the light. Another pup tumbled out, but the other two had to be drug out by their scruff at the back of their head. It was quiet up there on the hill, so the mother let her pups play in the sandy soil all day. The Father coyote showed up as the sun went down and slept on the landing outside of the den.

Another day arrived and the pups played at the mouth of the cave, tumbling down an incline and climbing back up. Mother and Father lounged in the sun and caught a few mice and voles to snack on. They laid the varmints in front of the pups who pawed them with fear at first.

After several days of sun, there was a big downpour of rain and Mother and the babies stayed inside. The Father disappeared for a few days, but he came back with the sun. One night, there was a full moon. The Coyote family came out and wandered around the rock formation. On the other side were four rabbits. Father Coyote dashed over to the little bunny and snapped his neck. He howled, the bunny cried a baby wail, and the pups danced over the dead rabbit, yipping the whole time. They repeated this routine for a few days and then one morning, the coyote family were ready to leave their nest and hit the Coyote Highway.

The next day was hot and Mother was panting. She needed water. It was time to leave the den. Before the sun was even to the rocks, the father and mother one in front, one behind, lead the pups down the hill. When they got to the edge of the woods, it was slow going, snaking around tall sword ferns and bushes. The little pups were engulfed way over their heads with vegetation. Soon, they could hear a dripping sound—running water of a creek. Cedar Creek, to be exact. Mother and Father drank long and hard from the creek. The pups stuck out their tongues to touch the cold water. They followed the creek and the creek got deeper and deeper. There was a tall bank looming down the hill. There was a huge hemlock tree down that was twisted over on its side. The Coyotes stayed under the tree for a couple of days in the cool forest near the creek.

The Coyote Highway was not a road or even a path. It was laid out along the creeks. There was Cedar Creek going down the mountain which led into and second branch of Cedar Creek, another creek, Goose Creek, joined Cedar, which connected to Chicken Creek, where one branch led into the Tualatin River and the other into Rock Creek and then into the river. From there, the highway was the Tualatin River, going into another river (the Willamette) and then into the Columbia River that entered the sea.

The coyote parents, under the downed tree, taught their pups to catch small animals. Their fur was thick and dark. As the summer stretched on into longer days, their fur turned lighter. They looked like wolves, but they had longer, floppy ears. Their skull is larger than a wolf, but their face and nose are longer. The coyote's body is very slim.

Some limbs snapped not too far away. It was a cougar, pouncing on a grey squirrel. The father coyote jumped up to see, then cowered down. But the cougar, who missed his lunch could smell some juicy coyote pups. Two of the little pups came up to the father. He grabbed them by the scruff and ran in a galloping style with his tail between his legs. Meanwhile, the mother coyote took off across the creek and into a field. Cougar went after the father who was charging along the other side of the creek. After a while, he was tired following the coyote and his meandering path that was going in the opposite direction of the Cougar's goal. He was headed up Parrott Mountain to the rocky out-cropping on the south side.

Father coyote let out a yip which was answered by Mother's yip in a towering blackberry bush. Finally, the frantic family was back together. At dawn, the group wandered out into the field. At one corner, there was an old sink full of water. They drank some water and then saw a line of cows coming their way, so they went back to the blackberry bush. It was a hot day and the coyotes were dehydrated by that night. They crept back to the water. The sink was only an inch deep and the pups, looking for more water started playing with a green snake, which was really a water hose.

They bit the snake and water came pouring out, they bit it several times and a spray of water came out to wash the shocked coyotes' faces. Then it stopped. Another night was spent in the blackberry bush with a dinner of mice.

It was time to move on in the morning. Father went out to find the creek early, so they could get down the coyote highway. When he came back there was a truck and three humans in the field by the sink. They were looking at the hose.

"Dad," said the short one. "Your hose is leaking all over the place!"

The farmer went over and looked at it. "Something with some sharp teeth got this hose all-right. We are going to have to go to town and get some new hose and fixtures." They got in the truck and left. The coyotes watched from the blackberry bush. It was time to leave and get to the creek. Father led the way.

The Coyote Family inched their way down these wildlife corridors and met other animals. There was the spindly-legged deer and the steely-eyed cougar. The pups learned to keep their distance from most of the animals, especially the ones on two feet.

Finally, they came to the biggest, deepest creek of all. It was the Tualatin River. From there they stayed on the south side, but they followed the waterway up-river around oxbows and horseshoe curves down on a flatland where no one lives on, even today.

Silver Lining

"Every cloud has a silver lining." (Proverb)

A ballad about a story sung in the key of D-dog. No, there is no key of H-hog. D-dog I say! Oh, okay! G-goat. I will play in that key. Anyway, that the true love of my life was not really interested in me no matter how I tried, no matter what I cooked, no matter how I worked so there was no need to hitchhike up I-5 anymore risking my life to cars as I dashed across on-ramps or off-ramps. No, it was not working—not at all—so what should I do? I think I'm going crazy! (Que the overcast cloud!)

The next day, I was looking for things to make puppets out of; just going through garbage cans and dumpsters. There I found letters to college students from their parents with five, ten, and even twenty-dollar bills! The envelopes were glued closed, never even opened. I read them all and enjoyed the funny cards and the money was great.

I got assigned to go student teach way out past Springfield which was fine with me except for the fact I would have to either hitchhike or take the bus or both. It was okay because the school nurse also traveled out that way and even though we were late to work, sometimes, no one seemed to care out there. I brought out my guitar and played for the kids. I made a great World Series bulletin board. Some guy hit a record number of home runs that went on the display. There was a lot of baseball books and they all got checked out.

One day I went back to the university to get a paycheck from the university library and the lady behind the desk asked where I had been. I told her about my job out past Springfield and how it took all my time to get out there she said that a guy had been looking for me and I said, if he was tall, I was not interested, and she handed me my check and a peppermint candy.

"Are you sure?" She asked. "He looked pretty smart and cute."

"I am sure." I said, firmly.

The next week it was dark with a fierce rain and the buses were slow. The school nurse did not come out to the school anymore, so I was all alone going out to Thurston. On Tuesday the bus stopped before my stop and the driver said everyone off the bus here because this was the new end of the line. In shock, I got off and had to walk about two miles soaked to the bone. I entered the office, and everyone was mad I was late. I opened my mouth to speak, but no one wanted to hear me.

By the next Friday, I was pretty late all the time. The school said that I didn't have to come anymore. Slowly, I walked back to the bus stop but before I got there a man picked me up. He seemed nice and was going back to Eugene. He was a preacher and we talked about a lot of things including my bus problems and getting let off of my student teaching.

He said, "You need a car if you are going to work at a school."

That might be true, but I could barely pay my rent, all my college money was gone. I did not tell him that though, because I was suddenly tired of trying to explain my problems. He pulled over when we got to town and I thought it was time to bail out of the car, but he put his hand on my arm and said, "I want you to use this money for something good to benefit a lot of people." He handed me a fifty-dollar bill.

I was sucking air and it was cold and I coughed: "I cannot do that!"

He was very convincing: "Yes, you need to help not one person but a lot of people, I insist. Surely a creative person like you can figure that out." The way he said it really made me want to do it. Blindly I got out of the car. Outside, the clouds were blowing apart and the sun shone through the clouds. All of them had a silver lining shining so bright it burned into my eyes. I said, thank you, but he had his head turned to the traffic and was busy trying to get back into the street. And then, he was gone.

I found myself outside a Safeway store so I went in and bought a bunch of food and took it back to my apartment and made a meal for all my roommates and friends. Of course, we had a music circle and sang the songs we all knew. All in the key of D and C and G. I am still a firm believer that every misfortune has a positive aspect. The old "closed door, another door opens" kind of thing. It's that silver lining around each cloud. That's what I'm looking for. That's my chorus and I am sticking with it.

Poor Old Boy

(This is a true story that happened between June 15 and the end of July 2019. It happened on the northeast side of the Oregon Coast range.)

Poor Old Boy bulldozed his way out of the rock pile. That is where he took his long winter nap. He had been there for four winter naps, ever since his mommy left him. Poor Old Boy sniffed the air. It was sweet spring. He was getting too big for his cramped quarters in the rock pile on top of Bald Peak. He looked down the mountain and could make out a big water puddle. It occurred to him that he could walk down to that mud puddle.

He got very frisky at the thought of drinking water and eating fish. His mommy gave him some fish once. He could go in that water and swim and not care a fiddle-faddle. He started walking on all fours in sort of a happy gallop. Sometimes he would lose sight of the mud puddle through all the trees, so he depended on his nose to smell the water.

Finally, after a day and a night, he found it and yes, that was where he was going to stay. The place was quiet and there was a path all around the big water. He jumped right in the cool water and then got out and dried his fur in the sun. Then he went up to a grassy bank and fell asleep. He had good feelings about the place.

The next day was sunny. Some shiny animals came down and roared around the trail. Then they came to a flat area with white lines. Men came out of the flashy animals. Later one of the animals, which had a baby tied to it, backed into the water. His Mommy had warned him long ago to not go near the shiny

animals or the men, so he just watched them. He thought the little animal was getting a drink, but soon the animal roared and the men got on top of him and they were all out in the water. It was scary, but Poor Old Boy stayed out of their way. Before they left, one of the men saw him on the bank. He shouted, "Oh look! There is a black bear!" Poor Old Boy galloped away into the brush. He did not want to see a black bear!

On another morning, he woke up to a large group of humans. Some were big and some were small. They brought out food and laid it on the picnic table. He could smell the fruit and meat. He went down to the picnic table to see what was there to eat. As soon as the humans saw him, everyone shouted: Bear! Bear! Poor Old Boy looked around but did not see this creature. The humans screamed and ran away to their hard animals. He had a fine lunch without them. He ate everything, then went off into the woods to take a fine nap in a bed of fresh sword ferns.

The Fine, Big Thing Made From Wood

Poor Old Boy lollygagged around in the ferns as the sun rose over the tall trees. Finally, he got up on his hind legs and looked around. From far away he could hear men talking about the trail of a bear. *This bear sounds like a frightening creature.* He thought. *I can hear the fear in their sounds they make.* He thought he should move on too to get away from this animal. He found a creek and walked up the mountain. He ate a few frogs. Finally, he found a rocky road and crossed it, plunging into the brush. He kept moving upward until he got to a flat shelf on the side of that mountain. There stood a fine big thing, like a cave. It was made out of wood, like a flat tree. He jumped onto the flat platform and looked out down in the valley. *What a nice place to be; to see over the land!* He thought. *This is where I will take my next winter nap. Right here in this wooden cave.* He raised up on his hind legs for a better view, and when he did, he leaned on part of the wooden tree opening and fell in! He bounced on a hard floor. He roared a bit in fear and grumbled around in the dark cave-like place. Poor Old Boy backed up and pushed the opening flap of wood with his hind end closing the opening. Everything was dark. He stumbled around and ran into another wooden thing like a picnic table.

Soon his eyes got accustomed to the dim light and he could see shafts of light coming in through the overhead of the cave. There on the wall, were some shiny things. He smelled them and there was a faint fish odor. He looked at one of the shiny things and there was a fish! Sure as shoot'en, it looked like a sockeye salmon! He bit the salmon picture, but it was hard. His tooth was stuck in the shiny hard thing! Fish juice went into his mouth. He grabbed the shiny thing with his paws and squeezed it, using his sharp can-opener claws to make holes. More fish juice poured out. He sucked on the can and more, rich, pink fish came out. He kept sucking and moving the can to get it off his tooth. It was good and very tasty. Finally, he wiggled the hard can off of his tooth. He finished the fish, but cut his paw, as he was startled from a roaring outside.

The roaring stopped and he could hear a few bangs. *Sounds*

like a human's hard animal!

Then he heard a real human: "Jerry, I thought you locked this door the last time you were up here."

"I did! I did!" said Jerry as he opened up a hole in the cave. Light came pouring in and the door slammed open against the wall. Poor Old Boy jumped to the sudden sound.

"I smell fish," said the man. Poor Old Boy dashed at the opening, right past the man. He wanted out of there. His tooth hurt and his paw hurt. He high tailed down the hill and never stopped until he got back to the creek.

Camp Poor Old Boy

Poor Old Boy nursed his wounds by the side of the creek for a few days. Then he thought about going back to the lake. He followed his nose and went right by another one of those flat-looking trees. This one had big white letters that said "Hagg Lake." He could not see them very good. The letters were fuzzy and sort of jumped around like ants.

He found a nice picnic table and set up his camp. It was on a bit of a hill, set back in the woods with a good view of the lake. No other humans laid out any food for him, even though they tried a few times. One boy came by and sat at the table with some sort of flat box in his hand. The box made a lot of sounds so Poor Old Boy thought he would take a good look. He leaned over the table and saw flashing lights and color. The boy looked up at him and started to scream. He dropped the box and ran. P.O.B. (Poor Old Boy) picked up the box with his claws. It was making lots of noise. He raised up on his haunches to look at the boy running down to the lake. He hobbled with the box after him with the box in his paw. Soon the box was all crushed and cracked, so he left it on a tree stump. It was making too much noise.

Most of the time, as the summer got longer, P.O.B. was all alone at his camp. Above the picnic table there was a berm of land with lots of sword fern for him to roll around on. He had fish, frogs, and berries to eat. He could even swim at night. On a Saturday morning, he would let the sun crawl high in the air and wait for the last people to find his camp. They would lay out their food and maybe run down to the lake. As soon as the food was out and the people were gone, he would bound out of the ferns to greet the people and have a picnic. He would hop onto the table in the middle of the laid-out sandwiches and bowls of chips and scoop up food with his paws. The people would scatter by running away back to their cars. The people were not happy with him, even when he opened their coolers for them and got out the cans. He just could not understand why they were so scared.

And why were those big dogs never friendly with him? Coyotes always romped with him, but not these dogs. He got into a wrestling match with one and the dog bit his paw. He yipped and ran off. That dog was not too good at wrestling.

The rangers chased him out of his camp. They finally chased him into a little metal house with wheels. They slammed the door shut. The metal house was hooked to one of those hard animals. One of the rangers said: "Poor Old Boy, I feel sorry for him. Look at him, he looks so forlorn." The other ranger laughed. "Don't be sorry for him, man. He is going to heaven on earth. We are taking him up to the Wallowa Mountains where there are many females, but very few males, the poor sucker. He is going to think he has died and gone to heaven."

And with that roar of the truck, P.O.B. was on the road, up Highway 84, to Eastern Oregon and bear country.

Part 2

Covid Times

We interrupt this book, because we had to, not that we wanted to. At first, I was not going to write about this world-wide pandemic, but now it seems fitting in a book titled *Overcast with Sunbreaks*.

There is a parallel theme both of doom and gloom and that of hope and brightness on the other side. I first heard about this Covid-19 threat on January 2, 2020 and right up to the publishing of this book, June 30, 2021, we are still struggling.

Over a year has gone by and we are wondering: "When will we get back to normal?"

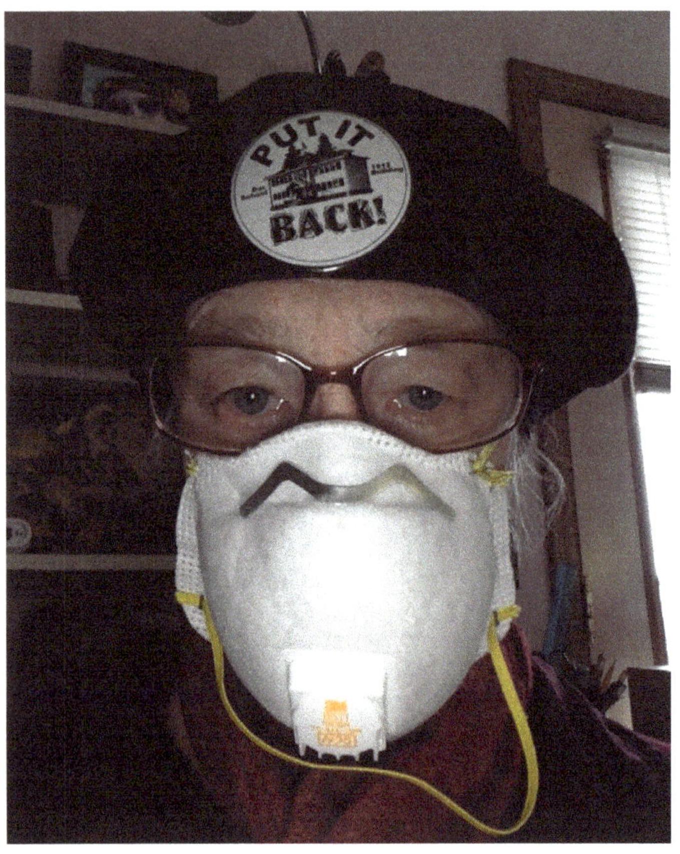
PUT IT
BACK!

Stranger at the door...

A gnarled man came to my door during the Covid Times.
He asked if he could come on in—to him I did decline.
I took him 'round the garden gate to sit upon the deck.
We chatted on about the times, of health, and his stiff neck.
He asked me for a piece of bread and a cup of water.
I asked, "How did you get this way?" He said it did not matter.
"You've helped me out," beamed the crooked man as he rose stiffly to leave.
"I've got a gift, a perfect prize, just right up my sleeve."
He looked out to my garden, my pretty flowered land.
Eyes twinkled for a second, he opened up his hand.
"The seed of life for you, my dear. Use it well, for it will end."
I helped him 'round the garden gate. My time to him I lend.
Our lives are not that different. Our journey we will spend.
I've often thought about this man and others that do roam.
They often go into the sun. They all walk there alone.

Weather Report

May 15, 2020

The only entertainment we have in these days of Covid 19 is the news and the weather. The programs on TV are boring and the re-runs are of reruns. Radio is not bad, but you can only take so much of the ads or the blaring music. Internet has slowed down to such a crawl that I forgot what I was going to write or look up. So now I am back to watching the weather both on TV and the big screen in the sky.

On the wide-screen TV in our hovel, there is usually a man or a lady, all dolled up, standing in front of a big screen with 3-D maps all over it. It almost looks like we are on a jet plane, looking down on mountains and rivers. There are extra charts and graphs. Then they flash another map of Oregon, all covered with grey clouds and bits of terrain peeking through the small gaps. There are town labels on top of the grey mass indicating there are places below.

The classy weather lady that my great aunt can't stand begins to hold forth. "Well, Oregonians, our weather is changing," she purrs.

Filbert, my half-deaf great aunt starts yelling at the TV. I jump because I forgot she was sitting in the dark corner. "Oh yeah? Fancy Nancy? You could have fooled me! It's spring, for Chriss-sake."

"How do you know what she just said?" I questioned. "I thought you were deaf."

"Huh?" says Filbert. You have to speak up my dear," she says in her sweet, feeble voice. I yell the question again.

"I just got my hearing aids cleaned," she said. These forecasters always say the weather is changing—day after day, until after the 4th of July. You just wait. They are going to go to commercial before you know what is really going to happen tomorrow."

Intrigued, I sat down in a soft chair that sunk clear to the floor. Sure enough, after ten minutes of ads—there was our weather girl. She waved her arms and magic sprinkles dashed across the screen. "Aaannd, so everyone, tomorrow, it will be overcast in the morning, transitioning to high clouds and sunbreaks in the afternoon." The weather person seemed relieved with this pronouncement. I, also breathed a sigh of relief.

"Overcast with sunbreaks!!" shouted Filbert. "This is the sixteenth day of this forecast and I've yet to see the sun." She marked another hash mark on her white board which was given to her at the hospital after one of her shouting attacks. "I want to see one more full day of sun before I die," she demanded. Her blood pressure was boiling.

"Now, now, Great Aunt Filbert. Calm down. A couple of days ago, the sun came out, but you were napping. You know summer really does not start here in Oregon until after the 4th of July." I patted her lightly on the shoulder.

She heaved a sigh of resignation. "Oh yes of course, my dear. We are in Oregon, not Texas. It's my own fault for following my husband Al out here to work on the Bonneville Dam. Should'da stayed where there was no water...Oh yes, I must be patient. That's what my caregiver, Julie, says."

"Well, Julie is a wise woman, Great Aunt Filbert." I struggled out of my captivating soft chair.

Suddenly, my seven-year-old grandson pipes up from

the gloom on the floor. "Grandma, how does the sun break, anyway? That sounds dangerous to me."

"Humm," I answer. "Maybe Great-Great Aunt Filbert can tell us—Great Aunt Filbert? You want to answer that question? How does the sun break? Great Aunt Filbert?" I look down and see she is asleep.

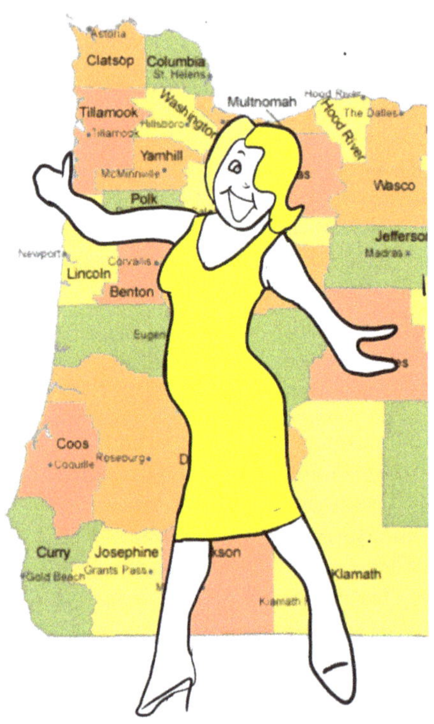

Dialogue

May 9, 2020

"A breeze of fresh air—that's all I want in this world. That's all I want."
"A good night's sleep," he replied.
She laughed. "A funny little boy with a smile on his face."
"A quiet rain to water this place."
"A rainbow of hope for love and grace.
That's all I want. All I want in this world."

Backyard News

July 3, 2020

Dear Aunt Gerry,

I writing to you from my home in Sherwood, Oregon. We are pretty much sheltering in place once again as the second wave of Covid-19 comes through. But beyond the foibles and follies of the human world, we have a backyard stage where a new state of activity exists. There are the usual suspects of scrub jay, robin, hummingbird, crow, and starling. Every time the sun comes out to swelter in the sky we see the ancient dragonfly soring in circles or the freshly-minted monarch fluttering about. We are lucky to live near a wildlife refuge that spills out to our backyard.

We have a new bird—the towhee, I call it, which is slowly populating our trees. The bird looks like an inside out robin, in a strange way, grey or white on its belly and orange on the sides of his body yet cloaked and hooded in black. The song of this bird is long, high, soft and delicately strung together by two or three notes. The bird is not showy, and just a tad smaller than the robin. Warbling wrens are also one of my favorite birds. Here in Oregon, they use our eve troughs as feeders, picking out all types of seeds and bugs. They will sit on the corner of the house, fill their chin pouches full of air and warble out a tune or two. They sing and call from every lamp post as I walk down the street: "All is well. All is well."

Now we are having even more activity at night. I have been soaking my feet out on the deck during the day and I left my foot bath out there. In the night two little masked burglars came up on the deck to wash their hands to the whole crime! This morning my foot bath is fogged by dirt and peat moss from the garden. They left their grubby paw prints on the sides of the tub, their delicate fingers almost showing their thumb prints. As I walked off the deck, I am confronted by five raccoon bombs strung across the fresh grass. They are all chock-full of cherry seeds.

I feel a bit bad about this and forgive them right away because my footbath is Epsom Salt that is used as a saline laxative for constipation. I hope they didn't drink too much of the water!

Well, I must close. I have a big cat scratching in the garden!

Love, June

Truck of the Barking Dogs

"A mystery is something of which we know what it is, though we do not know how it is." —Joseph Cook

July 2019

Historian Turned Detective

I'm not a gumshoe who sneaks around in the alleys looking for clues nor am I one of those G-men in their trench coats swooping down the stairs at the Morback Museum, but from time to time, I get involved in strange mysteries, or rather, the mystery chooses me. I am a historian by trade. There is a fine line between history and mystery. I get caught up in the middle of how and why things happen. No one else noticed the "Case of the Squeaking Floors," all over town or the "Mystery of the Moaning Stairs." There actually was a scientific explanation to those cases. No one even wanted to talk to me about the little girl ghost who knocked the tea set off of the shelf at the haunted Johnny Owens house. Luckily, my History Campers came to my aid, and we solved those cases with a little research and a real man from the FBI.

Now I've seen many things on the streets of my little town, but I think one of the most mysterious mysteries would be the "Truck of the Barking Dogs." I know, you are thinking—'that's crazy and not very interesting. Not like a carload of pokemons, or a VW van of circus clowns, or a truck of crazy, raving teenagers.'

Still there was something unusual about it to me, as I was walking down the silent streets of Sherwood, Oregon that first day. Picture it: these dogs are in a beat-up, faded red truck with a canopy and sliding glass windows with screens. The sound got my attention on those silent, Sherwood streets. The barking had a faint hollow, but consistent, sound. A half a mile away, something was definitely coming. The barking was punctuated with yelps and howls. I could see the dogs in the truck pressing their black noses into the mesh, as the truck rushed by. The dogs barked loudly, and the ring of their yelps was so echo-chamber-ish. It made me shudder for some reason. You could hear them coming and going like the Doppler Effect. The dogs I could see on the first day, in the windows, were all some sort of German Shepherd mix, from what I could tell.

I am not the only one to notice them. Other dogs in kennels, yards, and at the windows of neighboring houses heard them too and responded. They can actually use their dog-communication to bark at other dogs such as, "How's it going?"..."I'm hungry."..."Do you need water?"..."I need to get out of here or I am going to have an accident!" The dogs bark back on all the corners of the streets. "It's going great! I had a walk the other day!"..."I got a new bone!" "Three days with a dry bowl." "Hope it's gonna rain!"

The Dog Days of Summer

I see the Truck of the Barking Dogs every day that first summer, as the truck engine roars and the rattles down the street. The route of the truck seems to be on Pine Street, both going up and down. It is a long street which climbs a hill out of town that the locals call Washington Hill. The echo chamber of the barking dogs and the neighborhood reply is amazing, and yet no one seems to notice. I never see the driver because they have that smoked stuff on the windows. I keep thinking that if I can recognize the truck in time, I might be able to look in the wind shield. I make a note to do that.

On a Saturday morning, I sit on the front porch of the Sherwood Business Center, hoping someone will buy a history book. Two blocks up the street, I hear the truck coming with the barking dogs. The congestion from the Farmers Market has vehicles and walkers competing for the street. All the tethered-leash dogs are responding with rising tension, as the truck with barking dogs makes its way down through the intersection. Now is my chance to really see the truck, so I strain to see the driver. I can make out through the wind shield that the driver has a sharp nose, maybe a mustache, but that was about it. Then, through the side window, I can barely see that the driver has on a baseball cap. He looks kind of furry, like he has not shaved for a while. The truck rolls through the intersection, going way too fast. The dogs in the back are barking the whole time. Questions go through my mind: Where are they going? What are they doing? Why are they in such a hurry?

My "Chase Scene"

Then late, one afternoon, I walk out on Hall Street in front of my house. The red truck with the barking dogs is careening around the corner and shooting down the hill way too fast. I jump out of the way and at the same time, decide to get in my car and follow this truck.

The old streets in our town are not straight but winding. The kinkiest one is most aptly called Willamette Street after the old river which flows northward from Eugene to Portland. There are some class-act oxbows kinking here and there on that street. I was careening this way and that to stay up with the red truck. The streets merge here and there until they get to the intersection of 99 W and Edy Road. I expect that the truck will go onto the highway, but it doesn't. Instead, it shoots up Edy Road. This is familiar territory for me as I used to live up there as a kid. At the final stop light out of town, the truck runs the red light crossing four lanes of traffic.

I mash on the brakes and watch The Truck of Barking Dogs get away from me, but not for long. Edy Road is steep, and the heavy truck chugs up the incline. I catch up very soon. Then the truck careens around the corner at the intersection and races across the first ridge of Chehalem Mountain. We go deep into Wunderli Canyon and up to Mt. Home Road. There, the truck takes a left and goes almost to the end of another T in the road. The truck jumps a shallow ditch and drives into a clover field that has been harvested many weeks ago. I keep going down the hill on Courtney which is still partly gravel and swing around so I can park just off the road to be able to be facing the right direction to go back home. When I get parked, I see the back of the truck is opened and dogs are streaming out of the truck. There are all sizes, all types, all very excited, dancing in the short clover stalks. They race around the truck a few times and then disperse all over the field. Some of the larger dogs trot down to the forest at the edge of the field. I tried to count them all and I get to about fifty when I hear someone say: "Ahem. Uh Ma'am. Can I help you?"

As I turn, I jump because this old feller with a broad moon face was breathing down my neck.

I squeaked with fear: "Nnnnooo. I am watching the dogs in this field."

The old farmer squinted his eyes. "What dogs?"

I looked back. Not a single dog was around on the whole field. I regained some confidence, hoping this old boy will help me. I look him squarely into his little pig eyes. "Well, they came out of that red truck over there in the middle of the field, anyway." Luckily the truck was still there.

The farmer with the moon face bent down to look me in the eye: "We got a lot of flatlanders commin' up here and gawkin' at everything...."

I felt defensive and interrupted. "Excuse me, but I'm not a flatlander. I grew up on this hill when I was a kid!"

He was taken aback for a second. "Well, suit yourself," he said as he turned and walked down the road, waving his arm.

I kept watching. The truck did not move. There were no dogs in the field. The sun went down.

Mystery Fundamentals

I sat there thinking about this mystery and I called my husband Karl. "Where the heck are you, Janet? I saw you jump in the car and take off."

For some reason, I was trembling. "Remember, I told you about the Truck of the Barking Dogs?"

He coughed. "Uh yes, are you still on that? I thought you gave up on that crazy notion of…"

I interrupted. "Well, I followed it up to Mt. Home Road. It's still in the field."

"What's in the field?" he asked.

"The truck," I said.

Now he sounded a bit panicked. "I think you should get out of there, Janet. Where there is a truck, there is a driver and old trucks have gun racks. I think you have seen all there is to see and…"

"Oh, some of the bigger dogs are coming up from the woods!" I say interrupting him.

"Janet, will you listen to me? You are never going to figure out anything unless you have some evidence or witnesses. You need an eyewitness. And on top of that, why do you even care? There is no crime in the mystery and if it does not at least bleed, there is no lead." He really thinks my sleuthing is a bit of a waste of time. I try to think how I will get some evidence or an eyewitness. Somehow, this whole thing with the dogs is more like one of those ghost investigations at the Morback House. Something is "there," but there is no there—there.

That Night...

Later I wake up to two headlights beaming down on my car. I startle awake. There is a tapping on my window. "Kin I hep you?" said a voice. It was a Washington County Sheriff, badges and pins glittering in gold, with a blinding flashlight searching through my car. I rolled down my window.

"Oh crap!" I breathed. "Where am I?"

"Right off of Mt. Home Road, near the Courtney intersection," said the sheriff.

Now I was wide awake. "Oh, yes, sir, I am investigating a case. I've been following this red Truck of Barking Dogs. They are a traffic hazard...they even ran a red light down in Six Corners. This truck has been driving all around town for weeks down in Sherwood and today, er tonight, I followed them up here. Is the truck still out there in the field?"

The Sheriff actually went around the nose of my car and kindly flashed his overpowered flashlight out into the dark field. There was nothing. No truck at all. The officer shook his head and slowly walked back around to the side of my car.

"I'm sorry, ma'am, but I am going to have you get out of the car, and take a few tests, and do you have an investigation license? Naturally after a three-hour nap, I passed all his tests. I promised to look into investigation paperwork. He could not figure out an infraction code for parking near a field, so he let me go.

He handed me a card. "Next time you see this truck and it does something dangerous, get the license plate and call me right away with the direction of where it is going." I realized that the license plate would be a great piece of evidence. I promised I would, but three months passed, and I did not see the Truck of the Barking Dogs.

The Eyewitness

I told my dog-loving neighbor Carla about the Truck of the Barking Dogs. She thought about the story for a while and then said: "You know about that Disney story called *All Dogs Go to Heaven*"?

"Yeah," I said.

"Well, it turned out to be a mafia story, and really not that redeeming of a cartoon movie, but the core theme rang through: All dogs go to heaven." Carla continued: "When I was taking a walk, I saw that truck one day down on the corner of Willamette and Lincoln. It was forced to stop at the stop sign because another car did a quick California stop and rolled through the intersection. A little puppy squeezed out the cab window and plopped down in the ditch. The truck kept on going. I picked up that pup and took it to the house. It was really weak and sick and died by the next morning. I buried him in the backyard and all the time I was digging the hole, I realized that the dogs in that truck may all have been going to heaven. It is just a theory, but it made a lot of sense at the time."

I looked at her, sort of relieved. "Well, now that amazingly does make a lot of sense and the reason why all the dogs disappeared in the field up there on Mt. Home."

"Uh-hum," she agreed. "But let's just keep this between the two of us, Janet, because this is a mystery that is not totally solved."

Parking Lot Evidence

It was true. The mystery of the Truck of the Barking Dogs was not solved, although I had a witness and a theory. I needed evidence. Summer was almost over, and the rainy days of fall were coming on fast. One overcast day, I was mailing a package of books at the post office and when I came out, there was the red truck. I quickly took out a pen and paper and approached the truck from the back end. I nervously wrote down the plate—ORS DOG. Really? That plate seemed so fake; I could hardly believe it! I took a picture of the license plate with my phone. My foot slipped on some asphalt gravel and the dogs inside the truck let out a howl, followed by profuse barking. The truck started up and started to back up! I jumped out of the way just in time, but then the truck stopped, turned, and rolled towards me! I jumped to the side and back and the truck followed me! So, I ran around the side of the parked car next to the parking space and cowered on the other side, but the red truck took off out of the parking lot. Since I almost got run over, I felt I could report the incident to the Washington County Sheriff along with all the evidence I had. I looked for the red truck every time I walked, but months went by without a sighting.

A Clear View of Right and Wrong

On a crisp, sunny fall day, my son and I were hiking with the kids on one of the old familiar trails at Champoeg State Park. We were going to go to the old town site and then beyond to where the American settlers, the retired fur trappers, and the British traders voted on a provisional Oregon government—the first American government on the Pacific side of America.

Suddenly, on the trail coming toward us was a little old terrier, running without a collar or leash. That was an unusual sight, even in this farmland. As the dog approached my grandson, Ahny the dog lover, he called him and held out his hand, but the dog rushed past him. He just shot down the trail!

We approached the little town site that had been wiped out in the 1860s by a hundred-year flood. All that is left now is a grid of the town and signposts where the houses once stood. The land is flat and sits on a high bluff above the river. It is hard to imagine thirty feet of water rising here from the Willamette River. Now it looks like a hay field with thousands of mole hills. But there, right in the middle of this field, there was the Truck of the Barking Dogs! All around the truck were all types of dogs bounding through the grass! One of my grandsons was running away from the dogs in fear and the other boy was chasing them around, trying to catch one to take home. No human was around. No truck driver.

We circled the truck. My son shook his head. "Man, where are the park rangers when you need them? This truck should not be just off-roading anywhere!"

I felt righteous. "This is the Truck of the Barking Dogs." Rhy rolled his eyes, recalling the story. "What did I tell you, Rhy, this guy is just not right in the head and look at these dogs! They are just tromping around! They are loose and this guy has just abandoned them here. You just can't dump a bunch of animals in the middle of a state park, leaving them to roam around maybe killing chickens or giving rabies to someone or an animal."

Suddenly a dog let out a blood-curdling cry, followed by a chorus of barking.

This made us both nervous, so we rounded up the boys and headed back to our parked car. We took one more look at the field and realized all of the dogs had disappeared.

"What really gives me the creeps," said my son, "is that this guy seems to be abandoning these dogs, just like in the city where people leave kittens in a box in the park. That is just not right for any animal and some of those dogs do not look too good—like they are sick. Yamhill animal control will have to round them up."

"That is true, and I had not even thought about that. It is unethical and sort of shady, for some reason," I mused. "I'm going to call animal control right now."

"I'd be careful, if I was you, Mom." My son is always looking out for me. "This good old boy is up to no good on a large scale, not just a kitten box dumping. He has to be doing this for money or some other mysterious reason." Months went by and there was not a sign of the Truck of the Barking Dogs.

Shadow Sighting at Snyder Park

Then in March of 2020, during the days of Covid 19, I was having trouble sleeping at night. I would wake up around 3:00 am and could not get back to sleep. This happened night after night. One rainy, dark night I heard a truck barreling up Hall Street and I could hear some barking dogs! I bolted out of bed, got dressed and grabbed my raincoat and an umbrella. I headed out into the rain and started walking up hill. When I got to the first intersection, I paused and thought: *Where would he go at this time at night? How about the dog park on Snyder Hill?* I took the longer, but less steep, route to the park. I figured that this might be a back-door route to the park and I was correct, as I approached the old farm site that is now a park. There were fewer streetlights, but I could see that even the tennis court light was burning bright into the distance. I approached the back side of the dog park area to see the heads of bouncing dogs in the dog park enclosure. There was the truck driver, standing in the middle of this sea of moving dogs. I watched this scene for a while. Then I started filming it with my camera on my phone. I could only see the driver's shadow, but for the first time ever I could see that he was a lean man in a coat and pants that were too big for him. Some of his long hair was blowing in the wind. He bent down to pet a short dog and then a bigger dog jumped up on him. He seemed to be enjoying the contact with the dogs. He was looking over his herd.

I moved into a deeper, dark patch of shadows and watched for a while. The rain had soaked through my raincoat and was cooling my skin. I stepped back and a limb cracked behind me.

Suddenly there was a whistle and the dogs spilled out of the pen. They made a beeline right to the red truck down in the parking lot and jumped in the back of the truck which had the tailgate down. There was a strange yelping at the dog park pen and I looked back up the hill as I moved slowly into another patch of shadows. There was a problem for sure up the hill and the truck driver was having trouble getting one of those Doberman dogs to follow the others. The driver grabbed the collar of the dog and drug him down the hill. Halfway there, the dog lunged viciously at the truck driver and ratcheted down on his arm. A struggle of two shadows whirled around and the dog let go of the truck driver's arm and ran down off Snyder Hill. The truck driver wrapped something white around his arm and hobbled to the truck, but in his haste to get in the cab, he lost the white wrap onto the parking lot as he roared off, not even closing the tailgate of the truck. A few dogs leaped out of the truck as it sped away.

I walked among the dogs who whimpered and looked very old. I picked up the rag with a stick. The white rag was a large man's handkerchief, splattered with blood. Under the streetlamp, I read the monogram on the cloth. It read G.O.D. Oh this was so rich, I started to laugh. I looked over at the dogs, but they were all gone, of course. So now I had a theory, a witness, evidence, and even blood. So, I reported the incident to the Sheriff and met him at the Sherwood Police Station with my new evidence.

Three days later, the Sheriff called and said, "Well Janet, it seems that we finally have a case. For four years now, the dog pound was supposed to euthanize old and sick dogs, but the person in charge didn't want to do it, so this person at the dog pound paid this Barking Dog Truck guy to do the deed. He was supposed to kill them, but he would just round them up and let them go. The dog pound person just got fired and we are looking for the driver of the Truck of the Barking Dogs. The blood on the handkerchief is all dog blood, even though it was the dog who bit the driver. Go figure."

It has been nine months since this final investigation and now the case is a cold case. So, for now, we must close the case of the "The Truck of the Barking Dogs."

Reflection

January 23, 2021

In conversation, I have told this story to many neighbors. Some people say that this is another mystic ghost story that could never be solved. Some say this should be one of those stories for "Unsolved Mysteries." Others say I have too much imagination. Other people contend that this story is part of a conspiracy theory to upend the city council and place dogs in the chambers. I will say that the truck and barking dogs is not made up. I'd like to think that the truck and driver have gone to a higher calling somewhere else in this universe.

2020

Time Overcast

Unseen and floating on a puff of air the virus arrives from one coughing lung to another. Slowly, the new host is notified by a headache, a fever, the ability to NOT taste the garlic on the garlic toast.

Since January 2020, the awareness of impending sickness and danger scatters the population from the herd to living in isolation. Only a few years ago, this would be the beginning of a sci-fi novel, but now it is reality. Fourteen months have passed since the bad news was announced, but it almost seems like fourteen years.

Luckily, Mother Nature and the season of summer have not been changed too much by the pandemic. Wildlife has wondered where the people have gone and have even wandered into towns to see what happened. In Oregon, the overcast sky opened up and enveloped us with warmth, light, fresh air and dryness. It brings me joy as I bask on the back porch or work in the garden. The wonder of plants growing, flowering and fruiting has become a new miracle. Birds flying, bees buzzing and critters scampering are a wonder. Thank all ye gods and goddesses that the virus has not influenced nature! We revel in this thought.

But when the seasons change as they always do each year in the hemispheres, to the colder, wetter climes, we are forced to observe our inner strength. Not only is the weather overcast, but we also have another layer of overcast hanging over us from above. The virus. We could be mad and resentful, blaming our misfortunes on others. We could do nothing, be in denial, and or deny or defy reality.

Or we could look beyond ourselves and think of others.

We could use that inner strength to do things we have always wanted to do. We could be creative. We could be philosophic. We could exercise or walk. We could rest. How a person operates on those overcast days tells us a lot about their life.

Sunshine in our Hearts

People of 2020:
Please don't lose your faith.
Please don't lose your hope.
Please don't lose the love.
Especially not your love.
For we are not fading like an old pen out of ink.
No amount of neglect or hate can stop you.
Every day, do something kind for someone else.
It will add up to your strength and keep the sun shining in our hearts.

The Dark Times

September 7, 2020

On the last day of summer, we took a long hike at Willamette Mission State Park. It was a glorious day, a little dry for August, but still beautiful. The boys galloped like horses on the trail and climbed the split-rail fences. By the time we got home, however, a huge, dusty wind bellowed, ripping at our clothes and blowing hedges and trees to the ground. Wildfires sprang up all over the state. The Cascade Range went up in smoke. The towns of Talent and Phoenix, down in Southern Oregon, were burned. The McKenzie River and the Detroit Lake area were laid to waste. There was even a fire on the West end of Chehalem Mountain near us. My grandson facetimed me a picture one evening of the mountain burning. Over the course of a few days, the smoke rolled over the sky. At first it was white, but then it turned orange, then gray. Black ash came raining down and I had to take my canvas tent down.

The sky is a gray ceiling now. It is warm, but there is a constant fall of rain. There is no wind and a silent and veiled puff of fog saunters through the Douglas firs. This is the Dark Times of mid-November. My grandson compares the overcast weather to the smoke.

Long about afternoon, in between shifts in the weather, there can be an opening in the clouds, some gusty wind, and sunshine. Oregonians know it is their window of opportunity to get out there and walk or dash to the back yard to do something. In the old days, a bit of rain and overcast would not stop us from taking the bus to the big city, or going shopping at the Bi-Mart, or doing some thrifting at the local used stores. But not anymore. Between the pandemic, fires, civil unrest, and a national election there is nothing to do and nowhere to go and still, we have the long dark days of winter ahead.

For eight months now, we have been dashing around with masks, trying to avoid the plague, Covid 19. There is no place to escape it and borders have been closed almost the entire time. As soon as the weather got bad, we had one less place to go: outdoors. Now we are in a horrifying second wave of the infection and there is very little choice to do anything or go anywhere. Why is this happening? Sad to say, but some people do not believe that the pandemic is real. They think it is a hoax. Some people feel that their freedom is taken away by wearing a mask. What about the individual's freedom to live? What about all the people who do adhere to the rules who are waiting for things to get better?

My grandson keeps asking: When can we go to the library? Can we go swimming yet? Will we be able to go to school or see my friends? Are we going to go to Halloween? Can we go to the zoo? Can we go to the Chinese gardens I read about in my reader? When can we go someplace on the bus? Are we going Christmas shopping?

We cannot do any of this because we—the adults in our world—will not agree to do the simplest things in the world because of their/our "freedom." They also claim that our governor and state leaders have some sort of "hidden agenda" for some sort of domination. No one in their right mind would ever do such a thing now that over twelve months have gone by. It is not a cruel prank. People have suffered enough.

It was pouring down rain when my husband called. "Could you come and pick me up? I feel like I'm under a waterfall." I got dressed and drove off to get him. When I got to where he was waiting, there was an overarching triple rainbow! The sun was like a spotlight. The trees with their last leaves were glowing golden. We got back home, and the spotlight moved to the west. The rainbow drifted with it and the clouds started rolling back into their place on the ceiling. A moment's promise was in that rainbow, during these Dark Times. How will we ever break out of this cycle?

June Alice in Wonderland

November 2, 2020

I wonder.
Why am I in this dark hole of life?
Why am I stuck in this time?
To go neither forward or back.
To go neither this way or that.
To wait each morning in the dark for the dawn. Waiting is the only game in town.

I wonder.
Should I go out and risk my life today?
It would be fun to climb out of this rabbit hole.
But at what expense, to the horrors of death?
I could go down that merry path that seems so familiar and comfortable.
Even pass by that O'le Cheshire Cat. (God, I hate that guy...)

I wonder.
Is doing anything productive today worth it?
Maybe I should sit on a toadstool and watch the fools go by.
I'd puff my hookah like a certain immature insect in limbo-land who does not care.

I wonder...
Why should I make myself so small when I am so big?
I could be helping someone rake their leaves or at least make cookies.
Maybe I should go talk to the Red Queen and ask him to be nicer.
That's it! I will go out no matter how hard, no matter how dangerous, no matter how hopeless.
I will do something today with caution and calm and then I will not have to

WONDER.

Hard Heads

Juneteenth 2020

Hard Heads, marching down the street.
Unmasked and making America great again.
Crowd together and feel the love.
"Until I've been removed by death or incarceration, I am not leaving."

Hard Heads are marching down the street.
They rally at the round house in their red hats.
They fly their pretty flags but there is no goal.
"The proof is in the statistics," said the physician. "I remain waiting for the next two weeks."

The Sirens of Corona wail o'er the land at dawn.
My heart races; there is no relief.
Sirens warning of another life to pawn.
"The greatest error is not to move. Speed trumps perfection."

Big guns marching along in angry suits.
Some cloaked in night, others in daylight.
Lying and shooting blindly. Death warmed over.
"This pandemic has magnified every existing inequality in our society."

Hard Heads, marching down the street.
Unmasked and making America great again.
Crowd together and feel the love.

Sherwood Walkers

"Neither snow nor rain nor heat nor gloom of night stays these couriers from the swift completion of their appointed rounds."

I know what you are thinking: the Post Office motto. But this popular belief, which honors the American Postal Service, is very deserving. The words above, thought to be the motto, are chiseled in gray granite over the entrance to the New York City Post Office on 8th Avenue and come from Book 8, Paragraph 98, of The Persian Wars by Herodotus. During the wars between the Greeks and Persians (500-449 B.C.) the Persians operated a system of mounted postal couriers who served with great fidelity. The firm of McKim, Mead & White, which designed the New York General Post Office, opened the office to the public on Labor Day in 1914. One of the firm's architects, William Mitchell Kendall, was the son of a classics scholar and read Greek for pleasure. He selected the "Neither snow nor rain . . ." inscription, which he modified from a translation by Professor George Herbert Palmer of Harvard University, and the Post Office Department approved it.

This motto can be applied to a new generation of people: the Sherwood Walkers. In the 1990s and maybe even before that, there was a group called the "Sherwood Merrywalkers" who hung their hat on the Robin Hood legend and walked the sidewalks and trails all over Sherwood and beyond. They were still having walks even when I moved here back in 1999-2000. I always thought it was a cool group.

The group got smaller and I do not see much activity from them in the last ten years. However, in 2005, I decided that I would start walking to my job at Sherwood High. The unscientific idea would be that if I walked every day for three years, I would offset carbon emissions and I would fly off to

Paris for some serious culture infusion. I actually achieved that goal.

When I came back, I kept on walking. People always asked me: "Where are you going?" They all wanted to know. "I am coming and going to work," I would reply. I was all alone out there walking, but soon a few more people also joined in. There was a guy who came marching up Willamette Street every day at 7:30 a.m. as I would be going down. He smoked a cigar every day, but I noticed lately, although he is still walking, that he has not been smoking any more.

My husband started walking to keep up some physical strength from hiking in the desert in Arizona.

"Where is he going?" asked some of the people along the way.

"Down to the Post Office," I would tell them.

Soon I started seeing more and more people walking everywhere in Sherwood. Some walked in the morning to avoid the heat of a summer's day. Some would walk early in the evening. Some walked their dogs. Others walked their babies in strollers. In the winter, people walked in the fog. Some also walked in high tech rain gear. Some of the teenagers walked right in the middle of the street in their hoodies. The rain would sog-out the sweatshirt material and soon the garment would be sagging down to their knees.

Now, during Covid-times, we see more walkers than ever before at all times of day. It is one of the few things to do when you have been cooped up in your house or apartment for so long. Somehow you need fresh air and exercise. Right at the moment, we are in the second or third wave of the virus. (I have lost track, quite frankly). There is nowhere to go anymore. The library is closed, the museum is closed, all the saloons are shuttered. The restaurants are closed, except for take-out… bla…bla…bla Now all the walkers can do is walk in a loop around to the park and back home. Maybe get a donut if there is not too long of a line. It does not even matter what the weather is like, now that it is winter. You just get out there and walk. No matter about offsetting carbon emissions anymore. We are not allowed to go to Paris anyway. The motto remains with the new generation of Sherwood Walkers:

"Neither snow nor rain nor heat nor gloom of night stays these walkers from the swift completion of their appointed rounds."

See you on the sidewalks and in the parks around town, but don't ask me where I am going because I don't know anymore.

The Call

By: June Reynolds, Larry Sousa, Debbie Wilson, Linda Matz Easterling, and Clyde Ray List.

Rise up! Rise up, all people of the earth, with unity and dignity, yeah, you, yourself, go out and Rise up.

Let each person up and down the street or town greet each other and share the warmth of the sky and try to help each other. "Hello, what can I do to help you?"

The anger of our Dark Days must cease and we must not deny the inner strength we have learned: to be humble and yet be great. Crack open the door in our own way.

Rise up people and share your wealth in your heart and the warmth of your love for each other regardless of our differences. For the tide washes the shore and brings in new ideas and hope from somewhere upstream.

Rise up, people and be the change you want to see. Climb up that May Pole of renewal to the pinnacle of health and new growth. Overcast though it may be, it is time to let the light break through with a smile to bring hope, peace, and love to all people, so Rise Up!

LIVES
OLOR
NOT A
CRIME

About the Author

June Reynolds was born and raised in Oregon. June taught in public schools for 35 years in Oregon and Washington. She taught Pre-k through 12th grade in reading, writing and history over that time. She has written three local history books of the Tualatin River/Sherwood area and several young adult books and short story/essay/poetry books of the Southwest. June splits her time between Oregon and Arizona, and loves spending time with her family, including her children and grandchildren.

Printed in the USA
CPSIA information can be obtained
at www.ICGtesting.com
LVHW062113180823
755632LV00040B/928

9 781945 587757